The Mummy's Hand

The mummy's hand floats on water and opens all by itself!

1. Tear this page out along the perforation.
2. Cut out the mummy's hand.
3. Fold on the dotted lines, like this.

4. Get a cereal bowl and fill it with water.
5. Now put the mummy's hand on the water. Do it carefully so that the hand floats in the middle of the bowl.

Watch the mummy's hand.
In a few seconds, it will begin to open.
Watch the fingers move!

You can do this trick over and over. Let the mummy's hand dry out and fold it again each time.

Cut on the heavy black lines.
Fold on the dotted lines.

SPOOKY ACTION CUT-OUTS

by JAMES RAZZI

illustrated by BERNICE MYERS

SCHOLASTIC INC.
NEW YORK · TORONTO · LONDON · AUCKLAND · SYDNEY · TOKYO

In this book you will find
    King Kong—make him swing his arms
    Dracula—make him roll his eyes
    Frankenstein—make him tip his hat
    And 10 more Spooky Action Cut-outs you can make yourself!
It's easy. All you need is a pair of scissors.

Here's what you do:
Fold the page along the perforated line and then tear it out.
Cut out the pictures or shapes on the page.
Put the pieces together the way the directions show you.
Then—put your spooky cut-outs into action!

Remember: Cut on the heavy black lines.
              Fold on the dotted lines.

No part of this publication may be reproduced in whole or in part, or stored in a retrieval system, or transmitted in any form or by any means, electronic, mechanical, photocopying, recording, or otherwise, without written permission of the publisher. For information regarding permission, write to Scholastic Inc., 730 Broadway, New York, N.Y. 10003.

ISBN 0-590-31242-1

Text copyright © 1980 by James Razzi. Illustrations copyright © 1980 by Bernice Myers. All rights reserved. Published by Scholastic Inc.

14 13 12 11 10 9 8 7 6 5 4 3   3 4 5 6 7/8

Printed in the U.S.A

The Witch's Nose

When you fold the picture, you will find the witch's nose!

1. Tear this page out along the perforation.
2. Cut out around the picture.
3. Fold the top part of the picture back on the dotted line.

Now the picture looks like this.

Check to see if you have folded straight on the dotted line.
Then press down hard on the fold.

4. Now fold the corner back on the dotted line.

   Check the fold and then press down hard.

5. Lift up the corner you have just folded and fold it toward you this time.
   The witch has a nose!
   Press down hard on the fold.

Now you can make the witch's nose appear and disappear!

**Cut on the heavy black lines.
Fold on the dotted lines.**

Whooo's Afraid?

Look on the next page to see what is scaring the boy. The two pictures go together to make one Spooky Action Cut-out.

1. Tear this page out along the perforation.
2. Cut out around the picture.
3. Cut the slit. Here's how to do it:

Fold the picture in half the long way.

Cut on the heavy black line.

Open the picture and press it flat again.

Turn the page for step 4.

Cut on the heavy black lines.
Fold on the dotted lines.

Whooo's Afraid? Part 2

4. Tear this page out along the perforation.
5. Cut out around the picture of the pumpkin.

6. Put the picture of the pumpkin behind the picture of the boy and...

poke it up through the slit.

Pull up slowly as far as you can.

Boo!

Gadzooks!

His jaws open and close!

1. Tear this page out along the perforation.

2. Cut out around the picture.

3. Cut the slit. Here's how to do it: Fold the picture on the dotted line. Cut on the heavy black line. Open the picture and press it flat again.

4. Now cut out Gadzooks' head. Be sure to cut the slit.

5. Put Gadzooks' head on his body by putting the white tab into the slit. Push down a little to lock the head in place.

Move Gadzooks' head back and forth to make his jaws open and close.

Crrr-unch!

Cut this slit.

Old Rocking Bones

This little rocking chair really rocks.

1. Tear this page out along the perforation.
2. Cut out the shape.
   This is what you'll have.

3. Fold the shape on the four dotted lines.

Fold down here.
and here.
Fold up here.

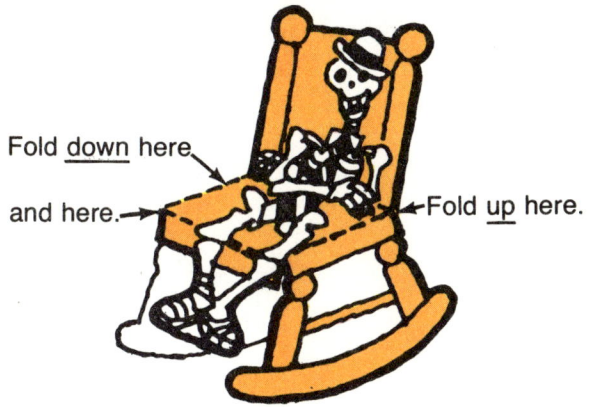

Press down hard on the folds.

Now rock the chair.
Rock those old bones to sleep.

Cut on the heavy black lines.
Fold on the dotted lines.

Give the Werewolf a Haircut

Before you start, think about how you want the Werewolf to look. (His hair will not grow back once you cut it!) If you don't want to cut off all his hair, curl it instead.

1. Tear this page out along the perforation.

2. Cut out around the picture of the Werewolf.

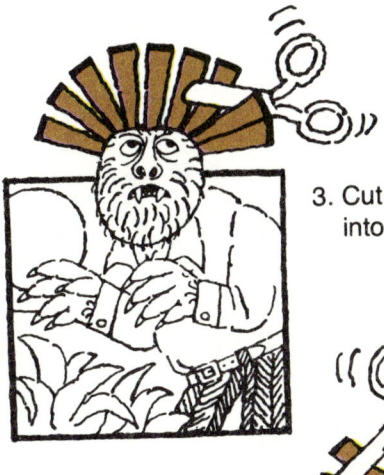

3. Cut his hair into strips.

4. Now give the Werewolf a haircut!

What kind of cut will you give him? Here are some ideas.

To make curls, roll the strips around a pencil.

Dr. Jekyll and Mr. Hyde

Dr. Jekyll (say **Jek**-ull) **is a good man. But sometimes he turns into an evil person named Mr. Hyde. Put his hat on and make him change from good to evil — and back again.**

1. Tear the page out along the perforation.

2. Cut out the hat.

3. Cut the slit in the hat. Here's how to do it:

Fold the hat in half the long way.

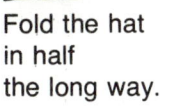
Cut on the heavy black line.

Open the hat and press it flat again.

4. Cut out around the picture of Dr. Jekyll/Mr. Hyde.

Put the hat on one side and you see the good Dr. Jekyll.

Put the hat on the other side and you see the evil Mr. Hyde.

Deadly Spider

Jiggle the deadly spider and scare your friends!

1. Tear this page out along the perforation.

2. Cut out the spider. It will look like this.

3. Now cut around and around the heavy black line.

4. Fold the red tab up. Fold the head down. The spider should look like this.

5. Hold the red tab and jiggle the spider up and down.

Eeek! A spider!

"Good Morning, Frankenstein!"

Frankenstein tips his hat to say "hello."

1. Tear this page out along the perforation.

2. Cut out around the picture of Frankenstein.

3. Cut the slit in the picture.
   Here's how to do it:

Fold the picture on the dotted line.

Then cut on the heavy black line.

Open the picture and press it flat.

4. Now cut out the arm.

5. Put the arm into the slit.

Hold the picture like this.
Hold the white tab and move the arm so that Frankie's hat is on his head.

Now move the arm up slowly—
Frankie tips his hat!
Move his arm from side to side and he waves his hat, instead.

**Cut on the heavy black lines.
Fold on the dotted lines.**

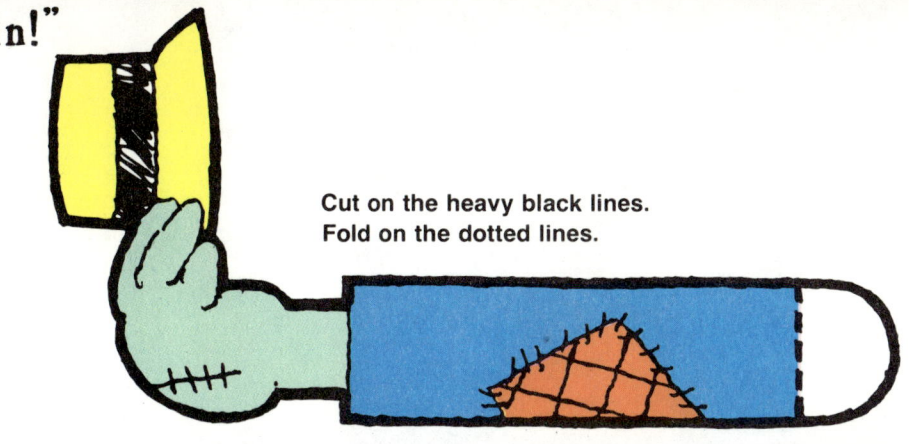

King Kong's Mountain

**King Kong's arms are on the next page.
Put the arms into this picture and
King Kong goes into action!**

1. Tear this page out along the perforation.

2. Cut out around the picture of King Kong.

3. Cut the slit on the right side of the picture. Here's how to do it:

Fold the picture on the dotted line.

Cut on the heavy black line.

Open the picture and press it flat again.

4. Cut the slit on the other side. Do it the same way.

Turn the page for Step 5.

King Kong's Mountain Part 2

5. Tear this page out along the perforation.

6. Cut out King Kong's arms.

7. Fold the red tab back.

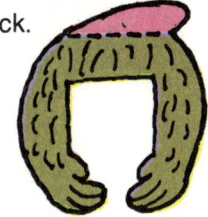

8. Put the arms into the slits from the back of the picture.

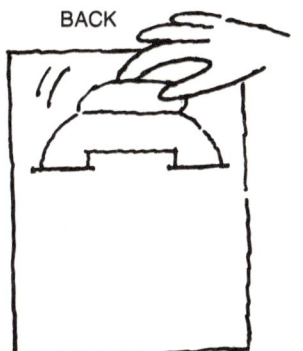　

BACK　　　FRONT

Hold the picture like this and make King Kong move his arms.

Move the tab up and down and King Kong's arms go up and down. Move the tab from side to side and King Kong's arms swing back and forth.

If you want to, cut out this boy and tape him to King Kong's hand.

Dracula Awakes!

Dracula pops up to surprise your friends.

1. Tear this page out along the perforation.
2. Cut out Dracula.

3. Fold Dracula in half.

4. Fold Dracula's head toward you. Fold on the dotted line. Press down hard on the fold.

5. Now fold Dracula's head back. Press down hard on the fold.

6. Unfold Dracula. Now fold him in half with the color side in.

At the same time, push Dracula's head forward so that it goes inside when you fold.

7. Now fold the two ends back.

Keep Dracula folded up and hold the ends together in your two hands. Then slowly move your hands apart— Dracula pops up!

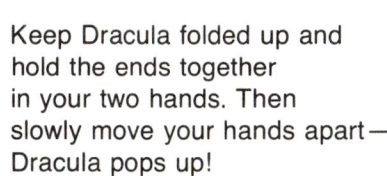

Hi, Dracula!

Dracula's Eyes

Put the two pictures together and make Dracula roll his eyes.

1. Tear this page out along the perforation.

2. Cut out the two squares.

3. Cut out the eye openings in the picture of Dracula.
   Here's how to do it:

Fold the picture on the dotted lines.

Cut on the heavy black lines.

Open the picture and press it flat.

4. Take the square with the eyes and lay it on a table.
   Put Dracula on top, like this.

Now move Dracula up and down and from side to side.
Do it slowly. Do it fast.
Dracula rolls his eyes!

The Ug

**The Ug's hand moves down, down, down...
and closes over the man on the raft.**

1. Tear this page out along the perforation.
2. Cut out the square.
3. Cut the slit in the picture.
   Here's how to do it:

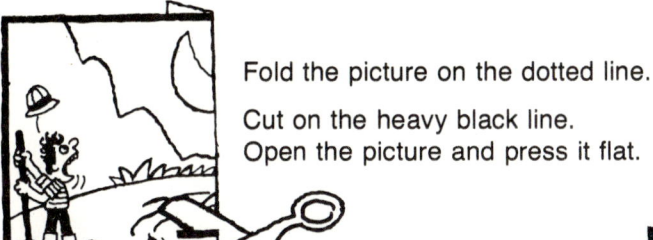

Fold the picture on the dotted line.

Cut on the heavy black line.
Open the picture and press it flat.

4. Now cut out the Ug's hand.
   Put it in the slit.

Hold the picture like this and—
move the hand down slowly...help!